RUTH HOOKER

MATTHEW THE COWBOY

Illustrated by **CAT BOWMAN SMITH**

ALBERT WHITMAN & COMPANY, NILES, ILLINOIS

Text © 1990 by Ruth Hooker
Illustrations © 1990 by Catharine B. Smith
Design by Karen Johnson Campbell
Published in 1990 by Albert Whitman & Company,
5747 Howard, Niles, Illinois 60648
Published simultaneously in Canada by
General Publishing, Limited, Toronto
Printed in the U.S.A. All rights reserved.
10 9 8 7 6 5 4 3 2 1

Library of Congress Cataloging-in-Publication Data

Hooker, Ruth.
Matthew the cowboy / Ruth Hooker;
illustrated by Cat Bowman Smith.

p. cm.
Summary: After receiving a cowboy suit for his
birthday, Matthew takes an imaginary trip out West
where he tames a wild horse, solves the puzzle of a
mysterious cattle brand, and captures some rustlers.
ISBN 0-8075-4999-1 (lib. bdg.)
[1. Cowboys—Fiction.   2. West (U.S.)—Fiction.
3. Imagination—Fiction.]   I. Smith, Cat Bowman, ill.
II. Title.
PZ7.H7654Mat 1990   89-21456
[E]—dc20   CIP
                                                   AC

The illustrations are ink and watercolor.
The text typeface is Clarendon Light.

To Matthew and his mother. R.H.
For Jeannine and Tom and their roadrunner. C.B.S.

Matthew got a cowboy suit for his birthday.

"A cowboy suit! Just what I've always wanted," he said.
He put on the boots and the chaps and the vest and
the ten-gallon hat.

"So long," Matthew said to his mother and father.
"I'm going out West to be a cowboy."

On his way out West, he came to a general store.

"Howdy," said the storeman. "I see you are a cowboy, but where's your horse?"

"I don't have a horse," said Matthew.

"That's easy enough to fix. The plains are full of wild horses. What you need now is a saddle, a bridle, and some spurs that go jingle, jangle, jingle. Here, partner—care to borrow these?"

"Don't mind if I do," Matthew said.

He strapped on the spurs, slung the saddle and bridle over his shoulder, and went jingle, jangle, jingle on his way.

When he reached the plains, sure enough, there were lots of horses.

A beautiful white horse came up to him. Matthew gentled the horse by stroking him and talking to him.

"Would you be my horse?" Matthew asked. "We can ride the range together, and I will call you Silver."

Silver whinnied. So Matthew bridled, saddled, and mounted him, and they rode out across the range.

Before long Matthew met another cowboy.

"Howdy, partner," the other cowboy said. "I'm Rocky, boss of the Rocky Nine Ranch."

"Howdy," said Matthew, "I'm Matthew."

"I can see you are a good guy," Rocky said. "I'd take it kindly if you'd come help me and my cowhands, Slim, Tex, and Pete. We've got trouble back at the ranch."

"Don't mind if I do," said Matthew.

Rocky handed Matthew a lasso. "Take this," he said. "You might need it."

"Thank you kindly," said Matthew, twirling his lasso.

They headed for the Rocky Nine Ranch.

On the way, they passed the Wagon Wheel Ranch. The ranch was full of cattle, all branded with the Wagon Wheel brand. Some strange branding irons lay near the fence.

"That's funny," said Rocky. "Where did all those cows come from? Last I knew nobody lived here at all."

At last they reached the Rocky Nine Ranch, with the Rocky Nine brand over the gate. Sad-looking cowhands were sitting on the fence. But there wasn't a cow in sight.

"Howdy," said Matthew. "I'm Matthew."

"Howdy," said Slim and Tex and Pete.

"Where are your cows?" Matthew asked.

"We can't find them," Slim said. "Last night they just plumb disappeared."

Rocky said, "There's dirty work afoot."

"Yep," said Matthew. "And I reckon the answer's at the Wagon Wheel Ranch. Let's ride."

When they got to the Wagon Wheel, the cows were gone. All they found were the branding irons.

Rocky said, "That's a mighty strange brand."

"It's not strange," Matthew said. "Put that brand on top of the Rocky Nine brand, and you'll get a Wagon Wheel. I'll show you how it's done."

Matthew drew a Rocky Nine brand. Then he drew the strange brand on top of it. Together, they made a perfect Wagon Wheel brand!

"You've got it figured out," said Rocky. "Let's get the sheriff."

So they took the branding irons and galloped off to the sheriff's office.

"Howdy, Sheriff," said Matthew. "We've got to catch some rustlers who've been stealing cattle from the Rocky Nine." He showed the sheriff the branding irons.

"I reckon it's Bad Bart and his boys," the sheriff said. "I heard they were back."

The sheriff made Matthew a deputy and gave him a star.

"They'll be heading for the border," the sheriff said, "but we can cut them off at the pass."

So they all mounted up and galloped to the pass.

They hid behind some boulders and waited.

Sure enough, they saw the rustlers heading toward the pass with the cattle. Bad Bart was in the lead.

"Ya-a-a-*ah*!" shouted Matthew. Twirling his lasso, he galloped right up to those rustlers!

Matthew captured Bad Bart!
Rocky and the sheriff lassoed the rest of the rustlers.
"You're all under arrest," said the sheriff.
Slim and Tex and Pete rounded up the cattle.

j41544

The sheriff put the rustlers in jail and gave the cattle back to Rocky.

Then the sheriff asked Matthew, "How would you like to be my deputy forever?"

"Thank you kindly, Sheriff, but the sun is setting, and I've got to be moving on," said Matthew. He handed his star back to the sheriff.

"Come and stay in my bunkhouse and be my head cowboy," Rocky said.

"Thank you kindly, Rocky, but I've got to be moving on," Matthew said. He handed the lasso back to Rocky.

As Matthew slowly rode away, he heard the sheriff say, "There goes the best cowboy in the West."

When Matthew reached the horses on the plains,
he unsaddled and unbridled Silver, said a sad goodbye,
and let him go to join the other wild horses.

At the general store, Matthew gave the storeman
the saddle, the bridle, and the spurs that went
jingle, jangle, jingle.

Then he headed home.

"Howdy," said his mother and father.
"Howdy," said Matthew.

"How about some grub?" his mother asked.
"Don't mind if I do," said Matthew.